An I Can Read Book™

The Horse in Harry's Room

story and pictures by
Syd Hoff

SCHOLASTIC INC.
New York   Toronto   London   Auckland   Sydney
Mexico City   New Delhi   Hong Kong   Buenos Aires

For Barry Joel, who thinks
his grandfather is a horse

ISBN 0-439-45492-1

12 11 10 9 8 7 6 5 4 3 2 1   3 4 5 6 7 8/0

Printed in the U.S.A.
First Scholastic printing, March 2003

The Horse
in Harry's
Room

Harry had a horse in his room.

Nobody knew.

He could ride him in a circle

without knocking over

the chair or the dresser.

He could jump him over the bed

without hitting his head

on the ceiling.

"Oh, it's great to have a horse,"

said Harry.

"I hope I will always have him.

I hope he will always stay."

His mother looked into Harry's room
to see what he was doing.
She did not see the horse.

His father looked into Harry's room

to see what he was doing.

He did not see the horse.

10

"Giddyap," they heard him say

when he wanted his horse to go.

"Whoa," they heard him say

when he wanted his horse to stop.

But they did not see

a horse in Harry's room.

13

"Let's take Harry to the country,"
said Father.

"Let's show him some real horses."

Harry did not care if he ever

went to the country.

He had his own horse in his room!

15

Every night

when Harry went to sleep,

he knew his horse would stay

and watch over him.

Every day

when Harry went to school,

he knew his horse would wait

for him to come home.

17

One day the teacher said,

"Let us all tell about something today."

One girl told about a dress

she wore to a party.

One boy told about a glove

he used for baseball.

18

19

"I have a horse in my room,"
said Harry.
"I can ride him in a circle
without knocking over
the chair or the dresser.
I can jump him over the bed
without hitting my head
on the ceiling."
The children laughed.
"Sometimes thinking about a thing
is the same as having it,"
said the teacher.

It was Sunday.

Harry's mother and father

took him for a drive.

They rode out of the city,

far out into the country.

Harry saw cows and chickens

and green grass.

And he saw HORSES!

"Look at the horses, Harry,"

said Mother.

Harry saw horses running.

Harry saw horses kicking.

Harry saw horses nibbling.

"Horses should always be free

to run and kick and nibble,"

said Father.

When they got home,

Harry ran right to his room.

"Horses should always be free
to run and kick and nibble,"
Harry said to his horse.
"If you want to go,
you may go."

Harry's horse looked to the right.

Harry's horse looked to the left.

Then he stayed right where he was.

"Oh, I'm glad," said Harry.

And he knew he would have his horse

as long as he wanted him.